MAYOR SLY
AND THE MAGIC BOW TIE
A KANSAS CITY ADVENTURE

HA CASS COUNTY PUBLIC LIBRARY
400 E. MECHANIC
HARRISONVILLE, MO 64701

AJA JAMES AND AUDREY MASONER
WITH KANSAS CITY'S MAYOR SLY JAMES
ILLUSTRATED BY ROB PETERS

ASCEND BOOKS
www.ascendbooks.com

0 0022 0503591 4

Story Copyright © 2017 by Aja James, Audrey Masoner and Sly James

ALL RIGHTS RESERVED. No part of this book may be reproduced or transmitted in any form by any means, electronic or mechanical, including photocopying and recording, or by any information storage and retrieval system, except as may be expressly permitted in writing from the publisher.

Requests for permission should be addressed to: Ascend Books, LLC, Attn: Rights and Permissions Department, 7221 West 79th Street, Suite 206, Overland Park, KS 66204

10 9 8 7 6 5 4 3 2 1

ISBN: print book 978-0-9989224-6-1
ISBN: e-book 978-0-9989224-7-8
Library of Congress Control Number: 2017942586

Publisher: Bob Snodgrass
Collaborator: Mark Fitzpatrick
Editor: Teresa Bruns Sosinski
Publication Coordinator: Molly Gore
Sales and Marketing: Lenny Cohen
Dust Jacket, Book Design, and Illustrations: Rob Peters

The goal of Ascend Books is to publish quality works. With that goal in mind, we are proud to offer this book to our readers. Please notify the publisher of any erroneous credits or omissions, and corrections will be made to subsequent editions/future printings. Please note, however, that the story, experiences, and the words are those of the authors alone.

The time-travel adventures with Mayor Sly James are fictional. All stories, incidents and dialogue with the exception of the real people and places that have been part of Kansas City's history are products of the imagination of the author and illustrator and are not to be construed as real. They are not intended to replicate actual historical events. Where real-life historical figures or places appear, the situations, incidents, and dialogues concerning these persons and places are entirely fictional and are not intended to depict actual events or to change the entirely fictional nature of the work. In all other respects, any resemblance to actual persons, events or locales is entirely coincidental. We hope you enjoy it.

Printed in Canada

www.ascendbooks.com

DEDICATION

This book is dedicated to all Kansas Citians, past and present, who have helped to make this city one of the best in the world. It is also dedicated to future generations who will continue to grow our city as a great place to live and work.

CONTENTS

It was a beautiful evening in Kansas City. Mayor Sly James had finished his day's work and was enjoying the view from his office. "What a wonderful city!" he exclaimed. "I am going to my favorite spot at the top of City Hall!"

He jumped from his desk and climbed the stairs to the roof. The moon was bright and the lights of the skyline were shining. "What a view! Kansas City looks magical! How fantastic it would be to travel back in time to explore its past."

POW! There was a flash! The Mayor saw a light coming from his bow tie. It began to spin and glow even brighter.

Then POOF! He disappeared!

Mayor Sly was now in a canoe floating on a river. Two men were in the canoe with him. There was open land all around.

"Excuse me, sir," he asked, "Where am I?"

"Well, you are on the Missouri River!" one of the men said. "I am Meriwether Lewis and this is William Clark. We are explorers. That high bluff would be an excellent place to build a fort."

"Amazing! My bow tie is a time machine!" Mayor Sly exclaimed. "And that high bluff is now Quality Hill!"

The Mayor had many questions for Lewis and Clark, but his bow tie started spinning and glowing. He was off again.

Standing in front of a familiar building, Mayor Sly exclaimed, "That's Kelly's! It's now on Westport Road. Kelly's used to be a general store for travelers heading west along the Santa Fe, Oregon and California Trails."

Walking into the store he heard a deep voice say, "I'll return tonight. I'm going to the City of Kansas for the day!"

"City of Kansas? I'm confused!" Mayor Sly said. Then he realized the man was John Calvin McCoy. McCoy established the Town of Kansas. It was later called the City of Kansas, and in 1889 it was renamed Kansas City.

"I'm remembering my Kansas City history!" Mayor Sly exclaimed.

Mayor Sly's magic bow tie whisked him away again. He was getting a little tired. He saw two women quietly talking in a hospital room. All the patients were children.

"Pardon me, is there a bed for a grown-up with a tummy ache to lie down?" Mayor Sly asked.

"Hello, I am Dr. Alice Berry Graham and this is my sister, Dr. Katharine Berry Richardson. You may rest here. Our Mercy Hospital treats only children, but we can give you something for your tummy ache."

"Thank you, but I thought the name was Children's Mercy," Mayor Sly said.

The two doctors replied, "Why, that would be a fine name for the hospital one day!"

Mayor Sly was soon feeling better. The bow tie began to glow and spin. "Oh, man, here we go again!" he said softly.

The Mayor landed on a green hillside. A big house sat on top of the hill.

"Hello," said a short, stout man with a newspaper under his arm. Mayor Sly jumped to his feet. He knew exactly where he was!

"You are William Rockhill Nelson," Mayor Sly exclaimed, "the founder of *The Kansas City Star*!"

"Yes, I am," Mr. Nelson said. "I am planning to give my home and land to the city. This would be a perfect place for an art museum. Maybe one day the museum will be known all over the world!"

Mayor Sly knew this was the future location for the Nelson-Atkins Museum of Art – and it **IS** known all over the world!

"Okay, bow tie, now I am going to tell YOU that I want to go to the Stockyards!"

Immediately the bow tie began to glow and spin. When it stopped, Mayor Sly was in the middle of the West Bottoms. There were trains everywhere and thousands of cows.

Inside the Livestock Exchange Building Mayor Sly saw people getting ready for an auction. This was early Kansas City at its busiest! Numbers on the chalkboard showed how many cows, pigs, sheep, horses, and mules had been sold that year.

"Two million cows in one year!" he read. "No wonder the Kansas City area is the home of the American Royal."

The bow tie began its magic, and Mayor Sly again went "POOF!"

"Mmmm, I'm guessing it's about 1920 in downtown Kansas City," Mayor Sly said. He saw a shop with bow ties in the window. "I think it might be time for a new tie after this adventure," he laughed.

"Can I can help you, sir?" a young man with round glasses asked.

Mayor Sly looked carefully at him. "Are you Harry Truman?"

"Yes, this is my store. Nothing special – I'm just a guy selling ties," chuckled young Harry.

"You have wonderful bow ties, Mr. Truman," Mayor Sly said.

"Please, call me Harry. It's not like I am the President."

Outside of the store was a young man with a pad and pencil. Mayor Sly asked, "Aren't you Walt Disney? What are you doing here?"

"I'm taking a break from my Laugh-O-Gram Studio near 31st and Troost. I've drawn a mouse character, but I don't know what to name him. Do you have any ideas?" Walt Disney asked.

Before Mayor Sly could answer, the bow tie glowed again. It took the Mayor to Liberty Memorial, where thousands of people were gathered.

"This is the dedication ceremony in 1926 for Liberty Memorial!" Mayor Sly said. President Calvin Coolidge had just finished speaking to the crowd.

"Hello, Mr. President," the Mayor said. "It is an honor to meet you. This memorial means a great deal to Kansas City."

"Pleasure to meet you, fine citizen," President Coolidge said. "The Liberty Memorial is the nation's monument for World War I. It honors the people who fought and worked for peace and liberty."

"Yes, it does," Mayor Sly said proudly. "We will always respect that memory. Thank you, Mr. President."

This time the bow tie took a shorter time hop, and the Mayor landed in the center of the Country Club Plaza. He walked by beautiful buildings that looked like they belonged in Seville, a city in Spain. A shop owner was hanging a string of lights.

"Need any help?" the Mayor asked.

"No, thanks. I am hanging the lights for Christmas," replied the man.

"Lights at Christmas are a great idea! Other store owners could do the same and have a lighting ceremony on Thanksgiving," Mayor Sly said.

As he turned to leave, his bow tie glowed and started to spin once again. "My next adventure awaits!" the Mayor shouted.

Mayor Sly found himself in a nightclub at 18th & Vine listening to Charlie "Bird" Parker playing the saxophone. The Mayor loved the jazz bebop sound, but he was hungry. Outside there was a mouth-watering smell. Mayor Sly left the club and entered an old trolley barn.

"Welcome! I'm Henry Perry," a man said serving a plate of delicious smoked meat and ribs.

The Mayor couldn't believe it. "You're the father of Kansas City Barbecue," he said.

"Haha! I don't know about that," Mr. Perry said. "Enjoy! If you want more, ask that fellow over there who works for me. His name is Arthur Bryant."

"Thank you," Mayor Sly said. But his bow tie started spinning and glowing again. "This is bad timing! I didn't even get to finish one rib!"

He landed in a nearby factory. "I smell something sweet!" Mayor Sly said.

"Would you like some candy? We just finished a batch of molasses chews," a woman said. "I'm Clara Stover. Welcome to Russell Stover Candies."

"Nice to meet you, Mrs. Stover. That's my favorite treat!" Mayor Sly said as he took a bite.

Clara chuckled, "These are made here in the Kansas City factory we opened in 1928."

"And I'm so glad you did! Yum!" Mayor Sly said.

He then turned and walked outside. As he took a breath of fresh air, the bow tie glowed and whisked him away to a seat on a wooden bleacher.

Mayor Sly was at Municipal Stadium at 22nd and Brooklyn. It was 1945 and he was watching a Monarchs' baseball game.

"Look! There's Satchel Paige on the mound!" Mayor Sly yelled.

Later in the game there was a loud crack of the bat. Mayor Sly looked up to see a home run! It was hit by Jackie Robinson, who would go on to be the first African-American to play in the Major Leagues.

Mayor Sly smiled as he watched these talented players. "Someday," he thought, "My friend Buck O'Neil, another Monarch player, will lead the charge to honor these men at the Negro Leagues Baseball Museum, right here in Kansas City."

He straightened his bow tie. With a glow and a spin, he was off again.

Mayor Sly landed in a vacant field on top of a hill. "Well, this doesn't look like much of anything," he said.

"What's that you say?"

Mayor Sly looked around and saw two men.

"Are you Lamar Hunt?"

"Yes, and this is my friend, Ewing Kauffman. We are planning to build two stadiums on this land. A new home for the Chiefs and one for Kansas City's new baseball team," Mr. Hunt said.

"I think that is a royal idea," Mayor Sly said.

"Royal. I like that!" Mr. Kauffman said.

Next Mayor Sly landed in a beautiful home where everyone was watching a football game on TV. He saw some of the players' names on the red jerseys: Bell, Taylor, Lanier, and Dawson.

"Welcome to Super Bowl IV!" the TV announcer said.

"Go Chiefs!" a gray-haired man yelled. "Glad you could all make it to my party! I'm J.C. Hall, founder of Hallmark Cards. We're on the way to a football championship for Kansas City!"

"This is a great party!" Mayor Sly exclaimed. "And you make a fine birthday card!"

As Mr. Hall's friends clapped and cheered, Mayor Sly's bow tie glowed a bright royal blue. He wondered where he was going next.

"The 1985 World Series?!?!" Mayor Sly asked excitedly. "Oh, it's Game 7 against the St. Louis Cardinals!"

He heard bat meet ball and looked up to see the baseball coming toward him. He reached up and caught it! It was a home run and the Royals took the lead. Seven innings later, Mayor Sly cheered loudly when he heard the stadium announcer say:

"The Kansas City Royals are your 1985 World Champions!"

"This is amazing! I'm so happy I get to re-live this day!"

Mayor Sly saw a familiar face jogging toward him. "There's George Brett!" he shouted as his bow tie took him away once again.

When he landed Mayor Sly shivered because it was so cold!

"Brrr!" he said. He was sitting in a soccer stadium with the fans chanting, "I believe that we will win!"

"Here!" The man next to him said, tossing a Sporting Kansas City scarf to Mayor Sly. Seconds later a shot was missed and the hometown fans went crazy!

Kansas City had won the 2013 MLS Cup!

Mayor Sly returned the scarf and uncovered his bow tie, which was already glowing to take him to one last stop.

This time he was in front of Union Station. Hundreds of thousands of fans dressed in royal blue held up signs and chanted, "Let's Go Royals!"

"I'm back at the 2015 World Series Celebration! We won!" Mayor Sly yelled.

His family looked at him and laughed. "Yes, we did, Grandpa!" his grandson yelled.

The Kansas City Royals stood on a stage with their World Series trophy talking to the fans. Confetti cannons burst and the crowd went wild. In the haze of blue and white, the Mayor was gone again.

He landed back on the top of City Hall, right back where he had started.

Mayor Sly walked back to his office. He leaned back in his chair and took a deep breath.

"What an adventure!" he said. "I met some of the people who made Kansas City such a great place. I saw many events from Kansas City's rich history. But I didn't see them all, so there may be a second trip!"

He looked at his bow tie, and it glowed with a sign of approval.

"Now, where should we go from here?' he said. "Perhaps to the future?"

MORE THINGS KANSAS CITY

Mayor Sly had a great adventure and learned lots about Kansas City history! But, there's more to learn about the places and the people he met during his travels with the Magic Bow Tie. Visit your library if you want to learn *even* more about our wonderful Kansas City!

American Jazz Museum – The Jazz Museum preserves Kansas City's rich tradition of music. The Jazz District area around 18th & Vine was home to many musicians of the 1930s and 1940s including Count Basie and Charlie Parker. Today the American Jazz Museum is in the same building as the Negro Leagues Baseball Museum on 18th Street. Its exhibits explore the history of jazz and the museum offers opportunities for research, education and performance.

American Royal – The American Royal began in 1899 as a cattle exposition and sale and was held in a tent. In 1905, a horse show was added. Today the American Royal includes a rodeo and a barbecue competition. Each year it reaches over 100,000 people who learn about agriculture through educational programs. The American Royal hosts over 2,400 contestants in nationally recognized competitive events each year.

Barbecue – Henry Perry is considered the father of Kansas City barbecue. He ran a restaurant out of an old trolley barn in the Jazz District during the 1920s and 1930s. When Mr. Perry died in 1940, brothers Charlie and Arthur Bryant took over the business. Arthur Bryant's Barbeque Restaurant carries on Henry's legacy today. Another of Mr. Perry's employees was Arthur Pinkard, who was the original cook for Gates Bar-B-Q.

Battle of Westport – This was one of the biggest battles of the Civil War west of the Mississippi River. It was fought along Brush Creek near the present-day Country Club Plaza and Loose Park.

Brush Creek – Brush Creek is more than 10 miles long. It starts in Kansas and runs through Kansas City, Missouri, before flowing into the Blue River. The Battle of Westport was fought along Brush Creek. Historic flooding in 1977 and 1998 occurred before changes were made to control the creek.

Cerner Corporation– Cerner was founded in 1979 by Neal Patterson, Cliff Illig and Paul Gorup. It is one of the largest health information technology companies. Its mission is to contribute to the improvement of health care delivery and the health of communities. Cerner supports its First Hand Foundation which gives money for children's health-related needs.

Children's Mercy Hospital – Two sisters, Dr. Alice Berry Graham and Dr. Katharine Berry Richardson, opened a small hospital for children in 1897. It became Mercy Hospital in 1903 and officially opened as Children's Mercy in 1917 at 1710 Independence Avenue. It remained there for 53 years until moving in 1970 to its current location on Gillham Road.

City of Fountains – Kansas City is known as the "City of Fountains" because it has more fountains than any city in the United States. The oldest city-built fountain still standing in Kansas City was designed in 1898 by George Kessler. It is called *The Women's Leadership Fountain,* and is located at 9th Street and The Paseo. Today there are 200 registered fountains in metropolitan Kansas City. Forty-eight of these fountains are publicly owned.

Country Club Plaza and Plaza Lights – The Plaza was built in 1922 and is the world's first suburban shopping district. Architects chose to design the buildings like famous buildings in Spain. In 1925 a strand of lights was hung above a Plaza building to celebrate the Christmas season. Each year more lights were hung and in 1930, the first lighting ceremony was held. The lighting ceremony is held every year on Thanksgiving evening. The Plaza Art Fair started in 1932 as a promotion to draw shoppers to the Plaza and to lift people's spirits during the Depression.

Crossroads Arts District – The Crossroads is a historic neighborhood between Downtown and Crown Center. Today Crossroads is an art gallery district and home to many restaurants. The area includes the former TWA Corporate Headquarters, Western Auto Building and the Firestone Building. The Crossroads Arts District hosts a First Friday event every month.

Crown Center – In 1966, Joyce C. Hall, and his son Donald, wanted to improve the neighborhood around the Hallmark offices. Their vision led to the development of Crown Center which is a shopping, residential, office, and entertainment complex. Hallmark's world headquarters is located at Crown Center. Crown Center is also home to Kaleidoscope, The Coterie Theater, Hallmark Visitors Center, the Ice Terrace – and so much more! Every year the Mayor's Christmas Tree is set up on Crown Center Square. Standing over 100 feet tall with more than 7,200 white lights, the tree's lighting ceremony is the day after Thanksgiving. After the holidays, the tree is cut into commemorative ornaments and sold to benefit the Mayor's Christmas Tree Fund which has been helping people in need in Kansas City since the late 1800s.

Ewing Marion Kauffman – In 1950, he founded Marion Laboratories which became one of Kansas City's largest companies. Mr. Kauffman was also the first owner of the Kansas City Royals and the Royals' stadium is named after him. Mr. Kauffman was very generous. In the mid-1960s, he established the Ewing Marion Kauffman Foundation. Kauffman wanted this foundation to change people's lives in Kansas City. The Kauffman Foundation has given millions of dollars in grants to support education, entrepreneurship and other causes.

Flood of 1951 – In July of 1951, heavy rains led to mass flooding in Kansas City and the surrounding area. President Harry Truman declared the flood as one of the worst the country had ever suffered. Over 500,000 people lost their homes. The flood damage was $1 billion which would be almost $9 billion in today's value!

Francois Chouteau – He was a fur trader in the early 1800s who had a trading post in Kansas City. It was called Chouteau's Landing and it was on the Missouri River near the north end of what is now Grand Avenue.

George Kessler – Mr. Kessler was a landscape architect who planned and designed boulevards and parks through the challenging landscape of the Kansas City area. His plan was part of the "City Beautiful" movement which began in 1893. In 1971 North Terrace Park, which Mr. Kessler designed, was renamed Kessler Park in his honor.

Hannibal Bridge – The bridge was built after the Civil War. It was the first bridge to cross the Missouri River and made Kansas City a major city and rail center. After a tornado damaged the bridge in 1886, it was replaced by the Second Hannibal Bridge, which is still standing today.

Harry S. Truman – After owning a men's clothing store in Downtown Kansas City, Harry Truman was elected a Jackson County official in 1922 and a U.S. Senator for Missouri in 1934. He was elected Vice President of the United States in 1944 with Franklin D. Roosevelt, and became President after Roosevelt's death in 1945. Truman was an important president because he brought an end to World War II. He and his wife returned to the Kansas City area and lived in their home in Independence, Missouri. The Harry S. Truman Presidential Library and Museum, also in Independence, was established to preserve the papers, books and other historical materials relating to President Truman.

H&R Block – In January 1955, brothers Henry and Richard Bloch owned a small bookkeeping business and helped some clients with their taxes. At the suggestion of an ad salesman for The Kansas City Star, they ran an ad offering tax services for $5. The next day they had an office full of tax clients. Henry and Richard named the new tax preparation business, H&R Block. Today H&R Block's world headquarters is in downtown Kansas City.

H. Roe Bartle – His full name was Harold Roe Bennett Sturdevant Bartle and he lived between 1901 and 1974. Mr. Bartle served as the Mayor of Kansas City (just like Mayor Sly) and helped Lamar Hunt move the Dallas Texans football team to Kansas City. Mr. Hunt renamed the team the Kansas City Chiefs after Bartle's nickname, "The Chief." There is a statue of Mr. Bartle at the Kansas City Convention Center which is also known as Bartle Hall.

J. C. Hall and Hallmark – Joyce Clyde Hall moved to Kansas City with two shoeboxes of picture postcards in 1910. His brother joined him and they opened a specialty store in downtown Kansas City to sell postcards, gifts, books, and stationery. When their store closed after a fire in 1915, the brothers bought an engraving and printing business which would eventually create greeting cards. A third brother moved to Kansas City, and in 1923 they formed Hall Brothers, Inc., which eventually became Hallmark.

Kansas City Athletics and Kansas City Royals – Kansas City's first major league baseball team was the Athletics, which moved from Philadelphia in 1955 and left for Oakland in 1968. With Ewing Kauffman's ownership, Major League Baseball awarded Kansas City another team the next year. Mr. Kauffman named the new team the Kansas City Royals. The Royals have won two World Series Championships – one in 1985 and one in 2015.

Kansas City by the Numbers – The city covers 319 square miles and is home to approximately 464,000 residents, making it the largest city in Missouri, both in area and in population. Its population is the 37th largest in the United States. The city lies within parts of four counties; Cass, Clay, Jackson, Platte and 15 public school districts. It is at the center of a 15-county metropolitan area with approximately 2,065,000 residents.

Kansas City Monarchs – Established in 1920, this team was the longest-running franchise in baseball's Negro Leagues. Before disbanding in 1965 the Monarchs sent more players to Major League Baseball than any other Negro League team. Famous players included Satchel Paige, Jackie Robinson and Buck O'Neil.

Kansas City Symphony – The Kansas City Symphony was founded in 1982 by R. Crosby Kemper. Its vision is to transform hearts, minds and communities through the power of symphonic music. There are 80 full-time musicians with the symphony. The Symphony has released seven recordings and won a Grammy Award in 2011 for *Britten's Orchestra*.

Kansas City Zoo – Located in Swope Park, the Kansas City Zoological Gardens opened in December 1909 with four lions, three monkeys, a wolf, fox, coyote, badger, lynx, an eagle and other birds. Today the Kansas City Zoo is over 200 acres and its staff cares for over 1,300 animals. Through its educational programs and exhibits, the Zoo connects people to each other and to nature by promoting understanding, appreciation and conservation.

Kauffman Center for Performing Arts – Opening in 2011, The Kauffman Center for the Performing Arts is at 16th and Broadway near Sprint Center and the Crossroads Arts District. It is the performance home to the Kansas City Symphony, the Lyric Opera of Kansas City and the Kansas City Ballet. The Kauffman Center also offers other programming including theater, outreach programs and community enrichment.

Lamar Hunt, The Kansas City Chiefs and Sporting Kansas City – In 1960 Mr. Hunt, a Dallas businessman, helped start the American Football League, which later became part of the National Football League. In 1963 his Dallas Texans team moved to Kansas City and became the Chiefs. The Chiefs played in the first Super Bowl and later brought Kansas

City its first World Championship by winning Super Bowl IV in 1970. Mr. Hunt was also one of the founders of Major League Soccer and formed the Kansas City Wizards in 1996. In 2010 the team was renamed Sporting Kansas City. It has won two MLS Cups – one as the Wizards in 2000 and the other as Sporting Kansas City in 2013.

Lewis and Clark – Meriwether Lewis and William Clark were the first American explorers to travel across the western United States. In 1804, on their return from the Pacific Ocean, they stopped in Kansas City. Today, a statue of Lewis and Clark is in Case Park in the Quality Hill area of Downtown.

Liberty Memorial – This is the original name for the tower and museum (located across from Union Station) honoring those who fought in World War I. It was dedicated on November 11, 1926, by President Calvin Coolidge. In 2006, the museum was expanded and is now called the National World War I Museum and Memorial. It is the official World War I museum of the United States.

Loose Park – The park is just a few blocks south of the Plaza at 51st and Wornall Road. It once was a golf course and became a city park in 1925. It is known for the beautiful Rose Garden, Loose Lake, and a cannon from the Civil War. In 1968, the park made international news when a temporary work of art was installed. The park's 2.7 miles of jogging paths and formal garden walkways were "wrapped" in gold nylon fabric following the design by the artists, Christo and Jeanne-Claude. It took three days and 84 people to sew together and lay the 135,000 square feet of fabric. *Wrapped Walk Ways* remained in Loose Park for 14 days.

Mayors of Kansas City – There have been 54 mayors of Kansas City since 1853! William S. Gregory, who owned a grocery store, was the first mayor when the city's population was only 2,500 people. Kay Barnes was Kansas City's first woman mayor and she served from 1999 – 2007.

McCoy's Westport and Kelly's – Reverend Isaac McCoy and his family lived in Westport in 1831. Westport was a good place to buy provisions before heading west on the Santa Fe, Oregon and California Trails. Kelly's Westport Inn was originally operated as a grocery store.

Missouri River – The Missouri River is the longest river in North America and goes through Kansas City. Lewis and Clark were the first explorers to travel the entire length of the river. The "Mighty Mo'" is important for Kansas City's shipping trade. It is the city's water source, and is a site for recreational boating and fishing.

Negro Leagues Baseball Museum – The Negro Leagues Baseball Museum celebrates the history of all of baseball's Negro Leagues around the country. In 1920 the Negro National League, which included other midwestern cities, was founded in Kansas City. The museum is in the same building as the American Jazz Museum at 18th & Vine.

Nelson-Atkins Museum of Art – The Nelson-Atkins Museum of Art is an art museum that is famous all over the world and currently maintains a collection of more than 35,000 works of art. Started by the William Rockhill Nelson Trust and a legacy from Mary McAfee Atkins, the Nelson-Atkins Museum has over 500,000 visitors every year. The Bloch Building was added to the Nelson-Atkins in 2007 to increase gallery and storage space for the Museum. The Donald J. Hall Sculpture Park began in 1986 on the land surrounding the Museum. *Shuttlecocks* was designed specifically for the Sculpture Park.

R.A. Long, Kansas City Museum and Longview Farms – R.A. Long, who lived from 1850 until 1934, owned many businesses including a lumber company. He also donated to local charities. His home is now the Kansas City Museum. Mr. Long's country estate, Longview Mansion, hosts many events and a community college was also built on his land.

River Market and Arabia Steamboat Museum – The River Market neighborhood along the Missouri River north of downtown includes the area in which Kansas City was first founded in the mid-1800s. Originally it was called Westport Landing because of the dock for boats which brought goods for the trading post at Westport operated by Reverend Isaac McCoy and his son, John Calvin. Today there are businesses, restaurants, places to live, and the Farmers' Market. Also in River Market is the Arabia Steamboat Museum which displays artifacts salvaged from the *Arabia*, a steamboat that sank in the Missouri River in 1856.

Russell Stover Candies – Clara and Russell Stover made homemade chocolates and moved to Kansas City in 1925. The company continued to be family-owned until 1969 when it was sold, but its main office remains in Kansas City.

Sky Stations – When the Kansas City Convention Center was expanded, four 335-feet columns were built to support steel cables to suspend the Convention Center above the street and highway. Inspired by the Art Deco design of nearby Municipal Auditorium, in 1994, artist R.M. Fischer designed four different sculptural elements that top each of the columns. Each *Sky Station* was placed atop a column by a helicopter!

Sprint Center – Located in downtown Kansas City, Sprint Center opened in 2007. An Elton John concert was the first event. The arena seats more than 19,000 people. Along with concerts, basketball tournaments and other events, Sprint Center is home to the College Basketball Experience. The College Basketball Experience is an interactive entertainment facility where visitors can learn about the history of the game and visit the National Collegiate Basketball Hall of Fame.

Stockyards – The Stockyards were started near the railroad tracks in the West Bottoms as a place for owners of cattle, sheep, mules and pigs to sell their animals. At one time only Chicago's stockyards were busier. After the Great Flood of 1951, business at the Stockyards slowed. It closed in 1991.

Swope Park – This is the largest park in Kansas City and is named after Colonel Thomas Swope who donated the land in 1896. The park is home to a long list of attractions including Starlight Theater, the Kansas City Zoo, Lakeside Nature Center, Swope Park Soccer Village and Swope Memorial Golf Course.

Thomas Hart Benton – Thomas Hart Benton was a famous painter who came to Kansas City in the 1930s and began teaching at the Kansas City Art Institute. You may see many of his works at the Nelson-Atkins Museum of Art. Visit the Thomas Hart Benton Home and Studio State Historic Site to learn more about him.

Tom Watson –Tom Watson, born and raised in Kansas City, is a professional golfer on the PGA Tour. From 1975 to 1983, he won eight major championships (five British Open Championships, two Masters titles and one U.S. Open).

Truman Sports Complex – Named after President Harry S. Truman, the Truman Sports Complex is the site of Arrowhead Stadium for the Kansas City Chiefs and Kauffman Stadium for the Kansas City Royals. Arrowhead opened in the fall of 1972 and Kauffman Stadium opened in the spring of 1973.

Union Station – Union Station was a busy train station that opened in 1914. It closed in 1985 but reopened in 1999 with museums, exhibits and restaurants. It is the home of Science City.

Walt Disney – Walt Disney moved to Kansas City in 1911 when he was nine years old. In 1921, he opened Laugh-O-Gram Studio near 31st and Troost to make animated films. After moving to California, Disney said that a tame mouse that lived inside the Laugh-O-Gram Studio inspired him to create Mickey Mouse!

William Rockhill Nelson – Mr. Nelson helped people build homes and was one of the founders of the Kansas City Star newspaper. He planned for his home and land to be donated after his death to start a museum for the city. This museum is now the Nelson-Atkins Museum of Art.

Wornall House – John Wornall was a farmer and politician in the Kansas City area. His house was built in 1858 on his 500-acre farm and is now a museum at 61st and Wornall Road. It served as a hospital for wounded soldiers during the Battle of Westport.

18th & Vine – The 18th & Vine area is recognized as the birth place of Kansas City jazz music. Many famous musicians made this area their home including Charlie Parker and Count Basie.

ACKNOWLEDGEMENTS

From the authors:

Thank you to our collaborator, Mark Fitzpatrick, for his creativity and dedication to this story and to Rob Peters for his wonderful illustrations. A special thank you to Bob Snodgrass and Teresa Sosinski for their guidance and advice, helping to make this book something we can be proud of.

From Aja:

I would like to thank my family, especially my nephew Race, my niece Grey, and cousins Cruz and Mena, for being the joy and inspiration behind this book. I would also like to thank co-author Audrey for coming to me with her crazy idea to write a children's book. This has been a labor of love that would never have been possible without her vision and imagination. Thank you for being an outstanding co-author and friend.

From Audrey:

I would like to thank my family, Kevin, Carter and Mila, for inspiring this story. I would also like to dedicate this book to the memory of my Dad, John Masoner, who like Mayor James was a beacon of light in his own community.

From Mayor Sly James:

When I married my wife Licia, she agreed that if we ever had a daughter, we could name her "Aja" after my favorite song by one of my favorite groups, Steely Dan. I fell in love with the intricacy, time and rhythm changes of Aja the song and hoped for a daughter with the same level of beauty and complexity.

Twenty-five years ago, Aja Mackenzie James was born. She is the physical manifestation of the song — beautiful, independent, full of change, hope and rich rhythmic shifts. She honors me as the central character in this book written with her friend, Audrey.

Her mother and I couldn't be prouder of Aja and her entrepreneurial spirit.

"Aja, when all my dime dancin' is through, I run to you."